Tornado Tamer

by Terri Fields

illustrated by Laura Jacques

Mayor Peacock promised to save the town from any more tornadoes.

Everyone cheered. Well, everyone except Mouse. He asked, "Exactly how will you save us?"

"Why . . . uh . . . " Mayor Peacock didn't know. But he couldn't admit that. So he said he would hire a tornado tamer.

Then the mayor made posters. The birds flew them far and wide.

Weeks passed. No tornado tamer came. It was getting closer to tornado season. The terrible twisters might come soon.

Everyone began watching the sky for towering thunderstorms and strong winds turning counterclockwise. They worried their brand new buildings would fall. They worried their trees would be flung far away. They began to wonder if there even was such a thing as a tornado tamer.

Then a weasel arrived. "I am Travis the Tornado Tamer. I can make a very special cover. It will be big enough to protect your whole town."

Mouse spoke up, "But the worst tornado winds can get up to 300 miles per hour. Small ones can get to 70 miles an hour. Wouldn't your cover just blow away?"

Travis scoffed. "My cover will be made of magic threads. Put my cover over tall poles at the ends of your town. Tornadoes will bounce right off. You will be safe."

The cows said it would mean they wouldn't have to *mooooove* away.

The horses said, "*Neigh* to tornadoes! Yea to Travis!"

Then Mouse piped up. "Wait! Does this weasel even know how long tornadoes last?" Mouse turned to Travis. "Well, do you?"

Travis pretended to sneeze. He took a tissue from his pocket. He looked at the tissue and said, "The worst tornadoes can last up to an hour. But most last between one and ten minutes."

"Okay, my next tornado question is . . . "

"Hush, Mouse," the mayor interrupted. "We need Travis to start working!"

Everyone cheered except Mouse.

Travis said, "There is one more thing. Only those who are smart and special will see my cover. Otherwise, it will seem invisible. Do you think you will be smart and special enough?"

"Yes, yes!" the crowd yelled.

Travis said, "I can begin right now. But my fabric and thread cost a lot of money. You must pay me well."

"We will," everyone except Mouse shouted.

Travis took over the mayor's house. The animals left wonderful food at the front door. Travis said no one must bother him. He had to work alone.

Time passed. Every rainstorm worried the animals. They wished Travis would hurry.

Finally, the door to the mayor's house opened. Travis was much fatter than when he'd arrived. "I am finished," he said.

The mayor gave Travis a lot of money. Then Travis said, "I will bring out the cover. It is amazing. I hope you are all special enough to see and touch it."

Travis handed the mayor the first corner. Mayor Peacock did not see or feel any cover. But he was the leader. How could he not be special or smart enough? So the mayor pinched the air and pretended.

Soon, everyone was walking along holding their part of the cover—except Mouse. He couldn't see anything to hold. He sadly snuck away.

Everyone else talked about how smooth the cover felt. They said it was so easy to lift it up onto the poles.

Days passed. Even with the cover on, everyone could still see the sun, the moon, and the stars in the sky. They thought the cover was wonderful.

Then a storm of moist air from the Gulf of Mexico clashed with cold, dry air out of the west from over the Rockies. It twisted with warm, dry air from the desert southwest. Rabbit spotted a funnel coming closer and closer. Everyone dove into a shelter.

The funnel touched the ground and turned into a tornado right in the center of town.

After it ended, the animals came out and looked at the awful mess. "That cover didn't work one bit," Rabbit said angrily.

"*Baaad*," the sheep said. "We should have listened to Mouse."

Then one by one, they admitted they had pretended to see and feel the cover because they wanted to be special.

"Why that weasel!" cried the mayor. "Travis the Tornado Tamer tricked us!"

"He'd better explain himself! Where did he go!" demanded the other animals.

But Travis was far away. He'd found a town worried about earthquakes. The weasel was saying, "Yes, I am an Earthquake Ender. I can create a cover of magic threads. But only those who are very smart and very special will be able to see it."

For Creative Minds

Tornadoes

What if Mouse had been able to ask all his questions? Travis wouldn't have known the answers. The town wouldn't have hired him. So just in case some fake tornado tamer ever tries to trick you, here's what you need to know:

1. **What is a tornado?** A tornado is rotating, funnel-shaped wind. It connects a thunderstorm to the ground. Tornado winds are the fastest winds on earth.

2. **What is the damage path of a tornado?** It can be more than a mile wide and 50 miles long. But tornadoes don't always move in straight, predictable paths. They can destroy one house and not harm the one next door.

3. **Where do the most tornadoes occur?** Three out of every four tornadoes in the world happen in the United States. There's even a region called "Tornado Alley" that includes Nebraska, South Dakota, Oklahoma, Texas and Kansas. Some experts also include Iowa, Missouri, Louisiana, Arkansas, Mississippi, and Alabama in Tornado Alley. On average, there are 1300 tornadoes in the U.S. each year. Some years, there are over 1500.

4. **What time of year do tornadoes most tornadoes happen?** In the southern states, the most likely times are March through May. More northern states have most tornadoes from June through August. But tornadoes can occur at any time of year.

5. **What are waterspouts?** They are tornadoes that form over warm water.

6. **What color are tornadoes?** Some tornado funnels never become visible all the way between the cloud base and the ground. Often, a tornado starts off as a white or gray cloud. If it stays around for a while, the dirt and debris it sucks up eventually turns it black. A tornado's color also depends on where you are standing. If the sun is behind the tornado, you will only see the tornado's dark silhouette.

Weather Glossary

Clouds: a gathering of very fine water droplets or crystals that can be seen near the ground or in the sky. There are many different types of clouds.

Cold Air Mass: a large body of cool air that is either dry or moist. In the U.S., cool air is usually carried by wind coming from the West or south from Canada.

Cold Front: the leading edge of a cold air mass that replaces warmer air. The weather symbol is a solid blue line with triangles pointing in the direction the front is moving.

Funnel cloud: a rotating column of air (vortex) at the base of a cloud that does not touch the ground.

Pressure: a force made when one thing pushes against another—like when you hold something down. Gravity pulling air towards the earth makes pressure too!

Supercell thunderstorm: a rotating thunderstorm with strong air movement going up into the cumulonimbus clouds (updraft). This is the type of storm from which tornadoes form.

Temperature: how hot or cold things (including air and water) are. Temperature can be measured with a thermometer.

Thunderstorm: a rain shower with thunder and lightning. Often found where the air masses (or fronts) collide and always from cumulonimbus clouds.

Tornado: a funnel cloud that touches the ground.

Warm Air Mass: a large body of warm air that can be dry if it forms over land or moist if it forms over water. In the U.S., warm, moist air is carried in from the oceans or the Gulf of Mexico. Warm, dry air blows in from the desert in the Southwest.

Warm Front: the leading edge of a warm air mass that replaces cooler air. The weather symbol is a solid red line with half circles pointing in the direction the front is moving.

Weather: the condition of the air at a certain time and place including wind speed and direction, temperature, precipitation, and cloud cover.

Wind: the movement of air in a certain direction and speed. Wind symbols show how fast the wind speed (feathers) is and in which direction the wind is moving (arrow direction).

Wind shear: the sudden change of direction and/or speed of wind.

Vortex: a powerful spinning current of air or water that pulls things into it. You can see a water vortex when you flush a toilet or drain a bathtub.

Waterspout: a tornado that touches down on water instead of land.

What To Do If A Tornado Approaches

Tornadoes can occur in every state and at any time of the year. Before a tornado comes, you can be prepared by having an emergency plan. Know where to go for shelter. Keep a first-aid kit, water, and a battery-operated radio in your home and car. Learn the name of your county or parish and those nearby—emergency alerts announce tornado watches and tornado warnings by county.

A **tornado watch** means tornadoes are possible. If there is a tornado watch in your area, listen to the local radio or television for more news. A **tornado warning** means there is a tornado on the ground or that scientists who study weather (meteorologists) have found a possible tornado on Doppler radar. If there is a tornado warning in your area, find shelter immediately.

A good tornado shelter is a place where you are low to the ground, away from windows, and protected against flying or falling objects. Wear a helmet if you have one and put on your shoes. If you are near a basement or cellar, go there. If there is no way to go underground, find a room without windows—like a bathroom or closet—on the lowest floor and in the middle of the building. Sit under a table, desk, or strong furniture that can protect you from falling objects. If there is no furniture to sit under, crouch down on your knees and use your arms to protect your head. If you are in a car or a mobile home, try to get to a nearby sturdy building.

After the tornado passes, stay where you are until it is safe to come out. Look for people who might be injured or trapped, but be careful not to put yourself in danger. Watch out for fallen power lines and do not enter damaged buildings.

Enhanced Fujita Tornado Damage Scale

Scale	Estimated wind speed of a 3 second gust	Damage
EF0	65-85 mph 105-137 kph	*Light damage.* Branches torn off trees, small trees pushed over, and road signs damaged.
EF1	86-110 mph 138-177 kph	*Moderate damage.* Mobile homes overturned, moving cars pushed off roads, and roof surfaces damaged.
EF2	111-135 mph 178-217 kph	*Considerable damage.* Roofs torn from houses, mobile homes destroyed, cars tossed, and large trees uprooted.
EF3	136-165 mph 218-266 kph	*Severe damage.* Roofs and walls of houses damaged, trains overturned, and trees stripped of bark.
EF4	166-200 mph 267-322 kph	*Devastating damage.* Houses leveled, buildings blown away, and cars thrown significant distances by wind.
EF5	>200 mph >322 kph	*Incredible damage.* Strong houses destroyed and swept away, cars fly through the air more than 109 yards (100 meters), and high-rise buildings severely damaged.

Birth of a Tornado

Tornadoes develop over time. They follow a common pattern as they form. Match the vocabulary in bold to the photos.

A large, rotating thunderstorm, called a **supercell**, gathers in the sky.

A column of air starts to rotate horizontally under the supercell. This rotating air is a **funnel cloud**. It looks like a spinning, white or gray cloud. The funnel cloud can tilt vertically to point toward the ground.

The spinning air tightens. Like an ice skater pulling in their arms to twirl, the air speeds up as it tightens. When the spinning column of air touches the ground, the funnel cloud becomes a **tornado**.

A.

B.

C.
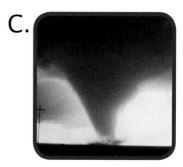

Photo Credit: The National Severe Storms Laboratory Collection, a publication of the National Oceanic and Atmospheric Administration (NOAA).

Answer: A-supercell. B-funnel cloud. c-tornado.

Make Your Own Tornado

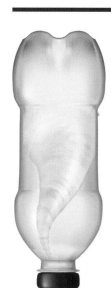

For this experiment you will need:
- water
- clear 2-liter plastic bottle with lid
- dish soap
- glitter or colored sand

Pour water into the bottle until it is about 3/4 full. Add a few drops of soap and some glitter or colored sand. Cap the water bottle tightly, so that you can flip it upside down without spilling.

Hold the water bottle upside down. Spin it quickly for a few seconds. Look to see if a tornado is forming (the glitter or sand will help you see it). It may take a few tries.

To my special Sweet Peas: Billy, JJ, Teddy, Danny and Vivi ~With all my love, now and forever ~Grandma—LJ

Thanks to Dr. Harold Brooks, Research Meteorologist with NOAA: National Severe Storms Laboratory, and Dave Williams, Chief Meteorologist at ABC's WCIV-TV (Charleston, SC), for reviewing the accuracy of the information in this book.

Library of Congress Cataloging-in-Publication Data

Names: Fields, Terri, 1948- author. | Jacques, Laura, illustrator.
Title: Tornado tamer / by Terri Fields ; illustrated by Laura Jacques.
Description: Mt. Pleasant, SC : Arbordale Publishing, [2016]. | Includes
    bibliographical references. | Summary: In this story based on The
    Emperor's new clothes, when Mayor Peacock commissions Travis the Tornado
    Tamer to protect the town, the weasel builds a transparent cover that he
    claims only smart and special people can see. Includes activities.
Identifiers: LCCN 2015035548 (print) | LCCN 2015041621 (ebook) | ISBN
    9781628557336 (english hardcover) | ISBN 9781628557404 (english pbk.) |
    ISBN 9781628557541 (english downloadable ebook) | ISBN 9781628557688
    (english interactive dual-language ebook) | ISBN 9781628557473 (spanish
    pbk.) | ISBN 9781628557619 (spanish downloadable ebook) | ISBN
    9781628557756 (spanish interactive dual-language ebook) | ISBN
    9781628557541 (English Download) | ISBN 9781628557688 (Eng. Interactive) |
    ISBN 9781628557619 (Spanish Download) | ISBN 9781628557756 (Span.
    Interactive)
Subjects: | CYAC: Tricksters--Fiction. | Tornadoes--Fiction. |
    Mayors--Fiction. | Animals--Fiction.
Classification: LCC PZ7.F47918 Tor 2016 (print) | LCC PZ7.F47918 (ebook) |
    DDC [E]--dc23
LC record available at http://lccn.loc.gov/2015035548

Translated into Spanish: *El domador de tornados*
Lexile® Level: AD 440
key phrases: adapted story (*Emperor's New Clothes*), trickster tale, weather, natural disasters, tornadoes

Bibliography:
"Fun Tornado Facts for Kids." Science Kids. N.p., 6 Feb. 2015. Web. 8 May 2015.
Spann, James. "How Do Tornadoes Form?" TED-Ed. Lessons Worth Sharing, n.d. Web. 11 May 2015.
"Tornado Basics." National Severe Storms Laboratory. NOAA, n.d. Web.8 May 2015.
"Tornado Facts and History." Missouri Storm Aware. N.p., n.d. Web. 1 May 2015.
"Tornadoes." Ready.gov. FEMA, 7 Apr. 2015. Web. 9 May 2015.
"Tornadoes." Weather Information for Kids. Weather Wiz Kids, n.d. Web. 25 June 2014.
"Tornadoes Fast Facts." CNN. Cable News Network, 7 May 2015. Web. 10 May 2015.
Watts, Claire. Natural Disasters. London: DK Publishing, 2006.
"Weather Ingredients." Web Weather for Kids. UCAR Center for Science Education, n.d. Web. 12 June 2014.

Manufactured in China, December 2015
This product conforms to CPSIA 2008
First Printing

Arbordale Publishing
Mt. Pleasant, SC 29464
www.ArbordalePublishing.com